The author, Cristian Biru, met a publisher at the Northern Railway Station in Bucharest during his studies in 1992 and accepted his works to be published for a modest amount of money each. Most of the Romanian books he would have published include in a rough translation: *Kikekoa-Crime Seminars*, *American Lighter*, *The Flesh Man*, *The Sand Knight*, *The Will of the Lazy Man*, *Waiting for Pain*, *The Romanian Teacher Book*, *Intifada Blues*, A *Bully in the Blues Pub* and A *Minor Course on Metaphor*. In 2015, he came to England for a better life, without being able to speak English. In 2016, his mother, Sultana Biru died and he had no money to come home to bury her. In 2018, his book, *The Sand Knight,* was translated into an Italian book under the title '*Il cavaliere di sabbia'*. In 2019, Katie Idle reads his short stories application under the title *Book Seller* and that is how this book came about.

I dedicate this book to my friend, Maria Dobrinoiu, who translated my heart into English. I also dedicate it to my good friends, David Dumitrel and Mishu, two special people who helped me bury my father in 2008.

For My best teacher,

Kate,

[signature]

29.11.2022

Swindon

Cristian Biru

BOOK SELLER

AUSTIN MACAULEY PUBLISHERS™

LONDON • CAMBRIDGE • NEW YORK • SHARJAH

A CIP catalogue record for this title is available from the British Library.

ISBN 9781398401730 (Paperback)
ISBN 9781398401747 (Hardback)
ISBN 9781398401754 (ePub e-book)

www.austinmacauley.com

First Published 2022
Austin Macauley Publishers Ltd®
1 Canada Square
Canary Wharf
London
E14 5AA

Many thanks to my dear friend Maria Dobrinoiu who helped me translate this book from Romanian to English.

Bag Lady

When he first came to New York, Ruslan was standing on the same bridge looking at the ocean. He was hungry and penniless, and he had no idea where he was going to sleep that night but he was young. The ocean had an irresistible colour that day, an iridescent blue shade, like a blanket full of gemstones under which a young couple was making love. The ocean had an indefinite, undecided colour now, somewhere between vomit and phlegm, a cardboard ocean winding around the bridge just like a puddle within an abandoned factory. An albatross flew back and looked at him. The bird hit the air with great strength as if it were clapping and moved away to the crammed barges of containers laid on top of each other on dozens of floors. Ruslan was under the impression that the bird was laughing while flying away. He quaffed the last sip of his vodka. The sun was rising above the glass like a gold coin. "Vodka never lies," he told himself, turning to the limousine that was waiting for him with its blinking crash lights. *I would have shared my last crust with him, had he asked me for any money*, Ruslan thought to himself, bitterly thinking of his friend, Iuri, who was now waiting for him at the company office, ready to deceive him.

He tightened his fur collar around his neck. Seen from the limousine, the traffic flowed steadily, calmly, quietly, just like a performance, but from the outside, the Brooklyn Bridge was threatening like the icy pipe of a revolver while the whistling cars were crossing in a fire exchange. As he threw the empty glass into the ocean, a tall woman carrying bags in each hand emerged from the traffic. The old woman was walking half-heartedly across the bridge and utterly surprised, Ruslan reached out his hand to warn her that a truck was just coming. Suddenly, the old woman caught sight of Ruslan. She stretched her long neck towards him and said something to him, but Ruslan only heard a kind of a hyena's groan. The old woman picked up her bags to strike her balance and the truck completely overlapped her. Ruslan took a few steps and lay on the sidewalk, trying to see the old woman's body between the wheels of the cars. The driver lifted him off the ground. Seeing his boss advancing with difficulty into the traffic, he grabbed his coat just as he was about to get crushed between the curb and the bonnet of a car that ultimately tried to avoid collision, disturbing the traffic further.

"I saw…an old woman. I think there was an accident."

"Where?" the driver asked, looking in the rear-view mirror. The traffic moved efficiently towards Brooklyn crossroads.

"Further on," Ruslan said, looking back carefully, sinking into the car's leather armchair. Surprised, he remembered how he was walking on the bridge like a disabled man rising from a trolley, trying to move his lifeless legs.

Looking at the driver's olive neck, Ruslan wanted to call his name, but he realised that he did not know him, although this driver had saved him from many critical situations.

"Hey, you," Ruslan said, "is your name Ahmed?"

"No," said the driver. "My name is Ridha."

"You are from Morocco, aren't you?"

"No, I'm from Tunisia. Can I start?" Ridha asked, surprised by the sweat bristles suddenly appearing on his forehead. His boss had never spoken to him that much. *I hope he just doesn't want me out*, he anxiously thought to himself, trying to figure out whether he had done anything wrong. His little girl, Halima, had just been admitted to college and the bank had asked him for a lot of loan documents.

"Are you married?" Ruslan suddenly asked.

"Yes."

"How many kids do you have?"

"Five, and I am thankful to God for all of them. I am the father of five girls."

"Five girls… But what's your salary?"

"Apart from the holiday incentives," Ridha said with slight embarrassment, "I earn $1600."

"According to your senior years?"

"No, that's how much I've earned since I started working here. $1600. There is no seniority in this firm."

"Is it a good salary?" asked the owner after a few moments of silence.

"It's not bad," Ridha said. "We can handle it."

"This means your wife works too."

"No, she does not work. She takes care of the children. She doesn't work. Arab women do not work, as a rule. We are not Arabs. We are Moustafi, a kind of Tuaregs," Ridha tactfully said.

"I just wanted to know…" Ruslan said after a few moments of silence, looking at his polished shutters that reflected his face like a mirror would. "How long has it been since you last went home in Tunisia?"

"Oh, I haven't been there long."

"Describe a dish you eat with your people there in Tunisia. A dish that reminds you of home."

"There are many dishes, but I particularly like a dish cooked by my mother. It's called the mouluhia," Ridha said, surprised that he couldn't help feeling overwhelmed. Ruslan sensed his emotion and became even more interested.

"What is this food like?"

"Oh, it's…a kind of green sauce that contains almost all known spices but also a rare plant, called mouluhia. My mother carefully picks it from the desert. In the middle of the plate, there is a piece of tender meat. We lay the flat bread on the plate and we all eat. The meat must be camel meat. If you do not cook camel meat, it doesn't taste the same; sometimes we use sheep meat, but that's not mouluhia anymore."

"From what I know, the Tuaregs consider their camels sacred and do not eat them."

"The Tuaregs are riders. And there are several species of camels. Some, which are white and tall, are used for racing, while some others are large and brown, and their meat is very tasty."

"Here's the problem," Ruslan suddenly said in a tone that demanded more attention. "You will leave me on the subway. You go to the office and take this business card to the reception. You tell them it contains a message on its back for the security chief. Call the chef manager and tell them I want to have lunch on the top floor terrace. I want to eat the mouluhia. If they don't bring my mouluhia to the table, tell them I'll kick them all out, all those working in the kitchen."

Ridha took the business card with the company logo and turned it over.

"It only has the letter O on the back."

"It's not letter O, it is a zero. The officer on duty knows better."

Coming off the bridge, the unusually long limousine slid elegantly down the freeway in the busy Brooklyn traffic, like an experienced skier on a crowded slope, leaving Ruslan at a subway stop. In the subway, Ruslan involuntarily smiled, feeling the crowd of people pushing him like a wave, luring him to the ocean. He remembered his mother when he left Orhei. He left her behind, standing in the doorway of their home, pulling himself from her as she was holding his arm and when he looked back, he saw through the door opening the corner of the table and the clay pots with milk, ready for breakfast. Sometimes in his dreams, sometimes in his waking moments when he waited at the traffic lights, this image kept coming back to him. *I will never do that again*, Ruslan thought to himself, remembering the moment when he threw the heavy crystal glass into the ocean, just to avoid carrying it to the limo.

He was reading the electronic panels while smiling, trying to find the subway route to the company. He stepped aside to avoid a group of students who pushed him slightly. A great number of worried, sweaty, absent-minded, tired, overworked, silent faces descended from a train. Heading to the station with a satisfied feeling, he reached the barrier and realised he had no money. A cashier looked at him strangely, assessing the value of his fur coat, his solid gold rings and his sparkling diamond watch.

"Can I pay by card?" Ruslan asked politely, searching his suit pockets.

The cashier threw an absent look at him and when he eventually made out where Ruslan wanted to go, he let him pass with a gesture as if he had let him go because a queue of people had already formed behind him, and until he had taken out his card and made the payment, it was likely that the queue would have doubled, as the cashier was not even sure that the card reader worked anyway and he had to make some settings that he wasn't sure he remembered.

"Thank you," Ruslan said and when he looked up, he saw the lady with the bags going down the escalator, careful about how to strike her balance, as if her bags had become too heavy. It really was her, coming down the escalator. Ruslan reached out his hand and tried to call her, only his chest stifled his call in a tobacco cough. Taking his hand to his mouth and coughing, Ruslan could see the old woman's face clearly, so clearly that he could search each of her wrinkles with a magnifying glass, or as if he were approaching the craters and the dry beds of a planet with a space shuttle. Her skin was like a slightly yellowed papyrus, a manuscript-like skin hidden in a clay jug within a cave. The elegant lady with the bags saw him and recognised him, glancing at him as if she were thanking him, and suddenly cried something to him. Her cry penetrated the space, as urgent as a spear.

Ruslan understood and nodded.

"Yes, yes," Ruslan replied, trying to rise above the wave of absent faces that were pushing him towards the subway train car. He was under the impression that he was jumping like a ball over those silhouettes, but he only tiptoed. His fur coat prevented him. It was warm but too heavy.

The wagon doors closed while on the other side of the neighbourhood, at the company's offices, Iuri was nervously talking on the phone. Next to him, his secretary arranged her hair and straightened her rumpled shirt.

"What do you mean 'he stopped on Brooklyn Bridge... with no apparent reason?' ...he can't have done that, maybe he met someone. He didn't meet anyone. He was staring at the ocean. No, no...follow him with all the people you have. What do you mean he went down the subway? Yeah...keep me posted, call me...no, not in ten, call me in five minutes."

Slightly worried, he looked at his secretary.

"Since I started working here, the boss has never come to the company using the subway. Today it's the first time. And that's a little weird."

"Yes, it's weird, but things are all in their place. Are the Japanese executives here?"

"They have been waiting for you in the meeting room for some time now."

"Have you checked the movie?"

"Yes, I have."

"He'll sign the contract. He likes strategic continental business. It's going to become worldwide now."

"What if he doesn't sign?" asked the secretary, stepping back slightly while feeling the Russian man's knife-sharp look.

"No, he'll sign it for sure. If I tell him, he will sign. I saved his life in Afghanistan. Make sure you look well. I'm waiting for you in the meeting room." *You idiot*, Iuri thought while coming out of the room, *if he doesn't sign, we are lost, we'll be loan shark's barbecue.* He tried to arrange the position of the chairs in the movie room once again, but he looked up noticing the restlessness. Security forces were placed at each door. The officer at the reception desk was checking his gun. He gave some orders through the station and the guards blocked each floor. An officer trying to take the elevator was lightly pushed to the waiting room and he dropped his files on the polished floor.

"What's going on?" Iuri asked a marketing assistant who had just spoken to a guardian.

"It looks like they received code zero."

The guards occupied the basement, the parking lot and a post right in front of the kitchen. The chef was just talking on the phone but there was too much noise because sushi was being cooked and fish was sizzling in the pans. When he suddenly shouted, his voice sounded like a shot and all the chefs stood still. Not even the fish sizzled in the oil.

"Yes, yes..." said the chef, "of course I know this dish, but...." The man left the phone and, with his sweat-washed face, told the people in the room who were waiting with huge eyes, "We need camel meat."

A few kitchen aides took the cabs that were waiting in front of the company to the Arabic stores in New York. To make sure he found camel meat in due time, the chef called a friend from the harbour master who assured him he would get as much camel meat as he wanted, as well as frog meat and monkey meat, if necessary; all he had to do was just calm down.

Turning off his cell phone, the captain resumed his work worriedly, saying, "What an idiot, how am I supposed to get him camel meat at this time? I need seven days for any order."

Iuri smiled trying to control his nervousness. He saw Ruslan's driver talking at the reception desk, looking at his watch. Suddenly, the manager appeared from an elevator, heading towards the meeting room. Iuri opened his arms wide to meet him, but he could not approach his employer. The guards discreetly but surely controlled the space around their boss. He saw the driver sitting very close to his employer, so close that he could whisper in his ear. Iuri wanted to make the driver stand from his seat or in any way make him realise that he was not entitled to sit next to his boss, but he bumped against the shoulder of a bodyguard who politely invited him to pick one of the empty seats and turning to the direction shown by the bodyguard, Iuri saw Ruslan's hand tapping the driver's shoulder.

The movie suddenly started and the room became quiet because the presentation was really effective, and the credits looked like the beginning of a SF movie. The satellites built according to a state-of-the-art Japanese technique were briefly presented, then a presentation of the profit that was very well done followed so that all the directors were watching the film breathlessly, while the secretaries sighed with satisfaction and surprise. The profit was a kaleidoscopic; it turned into charts, diagrams, geometries of success and eventually into rivers of coins and banknotes that bankers could barely manage to take stock of in their safes. While everyone was watching the movie, Iuri was looking out of the corner of his eye at the boss who seemed slightly distracted talking to the driver.

"It's not good," Yuri laughed nervously, "not good at all."

"Tell me, please," said the employer, leaning towards the driver's ear. "Next to the main door, there are two guards. Can you see them?"

"Yes," Ridha said.

"And a little further on, to the right, next to the window, there is a tall lady with some bags."

"By the window?"

"Yes."

"I cannot see her."

"It's no problem," Ruslan said, just as the movie finished and everyone applauded, excitedly turning to the boss. The applause suddenly got frozen. The boss looked around, looked at the doors, got up from the chair to be better heard and uttered clearly:

"I'll only talk once. Except for my driver, I want everyone out now," and as he said it, the guards were already forcing the crowd discreetly to the doors, so that the assistance came out orderly, calmly, as if it were a fire drill, leaving the head of the room to get closer to the boss.

"Mr Ruslan, your table is ready on the terrace, as you wished," said the cook, with an Asian accent.

Ridha sat down at the table smiling as it smelled like mouluhia. When he set eyes on a dish, his face lit up because the sauce had a vivid green colour, and when he brought the piece of bread to the meat in the centre of the plate, the meat sliced off naturally, as if a piece of ice were coming off an iceberg which went too far from the poles.

"Is the mouluhia good?" the boss asked.

Ridha closed his eyes, savouring the taste of meat in his mouth for a few seconds, as if he was tasting some old wine.

"It's perfect," the Moustaf said, and when he said this, the chef, who was leaning towards them waiting for the verdict, smiled and his smile passed on like a billiard ball through a half-open door, bouncing by the signs of the elevator guy, a guard and a receptionist, finally reaching the basement kitchen where the whole room burst into cheers, because all the shift had worked hard against the clock for this satisfaction, and they hugged as if it were the New Year's night, the cook's aides congratulating each other because they still had a job.

Turning to his boss, Ridha saw him talking with an empty chair and it was only then that he noticed that there were three pieces of cutlery on the table. Turning to Ruslan to his left, he saw the lady with the bags looking at him understandingly, waiting with her cutlery in her hands.

"You are my Death, aren't you?" Ruslan said, looking right into her eyes as if he had wanted to sense some shade of truth.

"Yes," said the old woman with benevolence.

"Then," Ruslan said, "let's eat; my death is very elegant and distinguished."

An oil tanker entering the harbour shook New York's landscape with the sound of its siren and the world vibrated as if shaken by an earthquake.

The Baby in the Bag

The story starts on a high-speed train. Yama Yamaha, a 21-year-old girl, took her seat holding a baby in diapers to her chest. The baby is sleeping peacefully; it has a very expressive adult face. If looked at closely, it is obvious that he has been through a great deal of suffering, even as a baby. Yama looks out of the window and she has the feeling that the train is not moving forward at all, just like a silver sword resting on a warrior's knees. But the train is going at a breakneck speed, scaring the birds in the Aokigahara forests. Hit by the branches of the trees and the steep cliffs, some dizzy birds fall like rocks near Saiko Lake, which the peasants call the Lake of the Suicides.

Looking out of the window, Yama catches sight of the look of a student lustily resting his eyes on her cleavage. In a split second, maybe due to the warrior instinct and her years of daily training, she briefly pictures a blow that would have more than likely fractured the student's throat; but Yama, though thinking of this deadly blow, smiles politely to the student and covers her plunging neckline, calmly getting her shirt straight.

Next to the student, there is an old woman who seems very irritated by the student's lecherous looks, and because he does not bother Yama, the old woman looks at her reproachfully as if her negligence has encouraged the student to behave like this. The old woman's eyes vibrate uneasily, spreading warnings, but Yama is very tired and doesn't realise it. When the student reaches out to introduce himself to her, she tells her name—Yama—and looks at the student as if she were looking through a glass. In fact, the student speaks to her for some time, confident in his wizardry through which so many girls have fallen that he cannot even remember them. And yet, Yama is absent. Her porcelain face and oblique eyes express serenity, but deep inside her, she feels crushed by stress and exhaustion as she has just given birth by herself a few hours ago, and now she is on a train with her baby, whom she intends to leave in Matsubase train station which is crowded and very close to the University Hospital.

The decision is already made, only the idea that she might again analyse the situation or the baby's fate throws her in a constant whirlwind of delirium, even though she has dissected this decision and turned its consequences over, endlessly debating inextricable details in her mind. The child would completely disturb the Yamaha family's business, which is rocked by the black forecasts of the financial markets, and her father would most likely not survive such disgrace. No, the baby should undoubtedly be dropped off at Matsubase station, just the way she had decided; she hasn't even named the baby to spare herself any regrets later, although she would have liked to call him Shintado. She avoids looking at the baby, afraid it would make her change her decision.

Suddenly, she is paying attention to the student who, while talking, is unnaturally leaning towards her, giving her a business card, hoping that one day the woman would call and meet him and when she sees how good, how passionate he is in bed, they would definitely become lovers.

"Oh," the student is saying, "Yama is an old name, very important in Tibet, because it is the name of the god of death in Buddhist philosophy. It is this god who binds the soul with a rope and leads it into the world of the dead. In order to understand the meaning of the name," the student continues happily, feeling the strength of his own language touching the woman's soul, "you have to know that there is a legend about Princess Savitry marrying a man about whose death she knew before he died, and the day her husband dies, he tells the princess he is going to the jungle for some firewood, but the princess follows him, simply knowing that her husband was going to die in a few hours. And when his time comes, overwhelmed with exhaustion and the feeling of death, the man sits on a boulder near a lake and he just dies in the princess's arms. Of course, God Yama appears, connecting his soul and taking him to the world beyond. Crying, Savitry follows the god and begs him to allow her man to live for at least one more hour because she hasn't managed to make him understand how much she loves him, but the god severely warns her that she is already entering the world of the shadows and there is no way to return to the Earth."

"How beautiful!" Yama exclaims in surprise.

"Yes, the princess spoke so beautifully to the god of death that he unleashed the man's soul and gave the man back to the woman, and her husband woke up on the stone in Princess Savitry's arms and they lived happily ever after…"

"It is a very nice story," Yama says while smiling as she prepares to take the student's business card, but when she bends down, her exhaustion suddenly pushes her forward, and slipping off her seat, she drops the baby into the arms of the old woman, who unexpectedly catches the bundle.

"Oh, dear, but this baby is in a shopping bag," the old woman says, surprised and worried.

Yama looks at her with a ceramic shocked face, but without expressing any feeling, she calmly responds.

"It is a special bag for babies."

"It's a shopping bag," says the grandmother reproachfully. "I take my morning vegetables in such a bag. Moreover, it is fat-resistant. Oh, dear me, but this baby eats while sleeping, poor baby," the old woman says, nursing him from a bottle. "You are lucky, girl, I was just coming back from my grandchildren in Kyoto." Taking the baby out of the bag, the old woman watches in awe the placenta traces on its belly and raises her face towards Yama, who snatches the baby from her arms to hurry to the exit while the train is still braking for the station. Then she turns and lifts her purse off the bench. The old woman freezes. She has the feeling that the girl has almost hit her.

"Strange girl!" says the old woman, following her figure with her eyes as it slowly vanishes among the travellers. "She said she intended to get off the train in Matsubase…"

Raising his neck like a giraffe, the student looks after Yama, thinking to himself, *such amazing legs, such wonderful body lines, such a beautiful figure, what an athletic woman. Now that I have given her my business card, I bet she'll call me tomorrow.* But when he looks down, he sees his business card on the floor, dirty from a footprint.

Yama quickly reaches a counter and picks up a luggage key. She finds herself in front of the cabinet and opens a box that reaches her chest, surprised while inspecting the inside, as it is too small for even a baby. But its interior is generous, except that she feels it might be too warm. Undecidedly, she looks at her baby who, while sleeping, is miming breastfeeding.

"Can I help you, miss?" a policeman asks in a friendly manner as he arranges his glasses, ready to introduce himself, but surprised, Yama almost slips when she turns her ceramic face, turning red at losing control. Blinking with her oblique eyes, Yama instantly says:

"I just wanted to get my bag inside, but…I have to go now," Yama says, speeding up among the throngs and disappearing into a train, the doors swiftly closing behind her. The policeman gazes in amazement after the train, wondering if the girl had been about to leave the baby in the luggage box.

The train Yama gets on is deserted. She moves with rapid steps from one wagon to another like a fighter getting by through the trees of a forest, controlling her breath. She enters a toilet. She puts the baby under the sink and washes her face. Closing her eyes, she concentrates on how she had felt during the first sword lesson her grandfather had given her as a child. She takes a deep breath, lifts the child and goes down to the first station, creeping like an invisible wave, like a wave of some flowing water through the roots of a steep bank, she reaches a counter, pays and takes the key. Heading towards the box area, she darts short, quick glances all around, discreetly assuring herself that she is not being either watched or followed. She opens a cabinet and leaves the baby there with such fine movements that even if she was being chased, nobody would have realised she had done it. Then she sits down at a bar and orders a cup of sake. She feels the alcohol cooling down her burning brain. The silence blankets her mind like a soft carpet of autumn damp leaves that her spirit is now treading calmly and pleasantly. Suddenly, she hears the child crying.

Restless, she hears the loud scream again, but strangely, everyone is passing the cabinet as if nothing can be heard. The baby's cry can be heard even louder this time and a couple stops, looking behind them undecidedly, but then they continue on their way, the man grabbing his partner by the waist, heading for a train. Yama jumps to the box zone and opens the cabinet, only now there is a bag with some sneakers within. She takes the bag aside and, in amazement, looks at the key which is clearly the one from the Matsubase station. Nervously, she reverses the bag and finally finds the second key among the things inside and opens a cabinet, only to realise it contains a briefcase. Yama takes the briefcase and throws it aside. An officer with a bunch of keys approaches, unable to understand what is happening, followed by two policemen.

"Quickly, open all the boxes, quickly," Yama says with emotion.

"What happened?" the officer asks, trying to support her because Yama has fallen down, confused and weakened.

"Open," Yama suddenly yells, and everyone stops moving, watching the scene as if a bang had sounded. "There's a baby there."

"What baby?" one of the policemen asks.

"A baby in a shopping bag..." Yama says in an exhausted voice.

Dog Island

One evening, the student was just descending the stairs of a restaurant on the cliff, when a woman responded with a smile to him looking at her glowing, melodious breasts like some baby deer. It was only then that the student, swallowing dry, recognised her as an old college mate, who asked him:

"Do you hang out with Orlando?" And because the student blinked in a puzzled way, the young woman added, "The painter?"

"Oh, Orlando, yes, he's…yes, he's my friend."

The student stared hesitantly at the woman who was entering the restaurant, surprised by the wide neckline of her dress but especially by the lines of her long thighs, her high heels, as if she were an athlete ready to start the race. He could barely remember her name. He had never seen her in an evening outfit and he had no idea there was such a centaur specimen among his college mates. During the university years she looked like a poor country girl who was commuting, and now she was walking like a pure-blooded Arabian mare on the steps of the terrace, gathering looks from the tables like a kaleidoscope of lasers. The student gritted his teeth, heading to the group of friends waiting for him at the bottom of the stairs.

Going down the steps undecidedly, he turned his head one more time, looking after the fabulous animal abounding in sexuality, who was walking as if she received endless love in her every movement, shining like an enticing electric advertisement in an ill-fated neighbourhood. The question seemed unnatural to him, and he found himself splitting up his senses as if he was removing the leaves of an onion in search of the truth. Had he considered her look, it was less a question than an alarming signal, as if she wanted to warn him, saying: "Be careful if you hang out with Orlando."

Why should I? the student wondered, walking along his friends and entering a beer house where. Someone gave the microphone to Orlando, who was just walking into the place, to sing karaoke to a song by Elvis, and when he started to sing, the room exploded in dance rhythms, while gorgeous girls, top models, started spinning around the students' table just like gemstones in a princess's necklace. Taking a mouthful of beer, the student felt his head unusually hard, and his neck instantly leaned to the table several times, until the student laid his head straight on his elbow and started snoring, realizing, however, that he was snoring and might fall asleep right there, and that it was very likely he would be awakened by the bartender while sweeping after the closing time.

Half into the world of dreams, he felt himself lift slightly, losing his gravity, and panicked holding the edges of the table with his hands. He might have raised his head to light a cigarette, or maybe Orlando had called him. Suddenly, he found himself turned by his shoulders by a girl who helped him hold the microphone in front of his lips, but he was holding her almost uncovered feet, highlighted by the sharp line of a coloured skirt. He may have even played a song, a

27

situation that scared him, because at that time he was not in a position to do so. His head turned into the table and he hoped he hadn't stood up from his chair. Closing his eyes, he realised that he had slapped a girl over her ass; though it was more likely that his palm had touched her wet side, making the dancer moan rebukingly. That was the moment when the student realised the tone of the question 'Are you hanging out with Orlando?' and he became sober.

I'm hanging out with Orlando, he thought, remembering that the previous day he had woken up in a car that didn't belong to him, and in no way was that supposed to happen again. Since he started hanging out with Orlando, space and time had become instantaneous, as if you could live in unexpected places on the planet, either one at a time or simultaneously.

Orlando explained to him that a friend in their group had put him on the back seat of the car, but he had forgotten him there, then the group left for a friend's wedding party in the city tower, where the state television office had been during the communist years.

He suddenly woke up in a bed in his underpants, surrounded by paintings and sketches; it was some sort of a workshop, and Orlando was just gluing some brass pieces on an iron door.

"I threw you in bed last night. It was very late and you were talking in your sleep. As you had no pyjamas, you slept in your underwear," said the painter, working at the door as if he excused the student for being nearly naked. "We're going to make some spaghetti," Orlando smiled, supporting his friend into the kitchen. "And some coffee."

The student watched the street from the balcony, realizing the dizzying height of the block he was in. In spite of the height, the street could be seen clearly, like a fresh valley descended by deer.

"Wow…" the student said, looking down the street. "I feel like I am in Colombia," then tapping his unnaturally round head like a basketball, thinking to himself, *although I have never been there.*

"I have a girlfriend from Mexico. I may bring her to Romania. I was really thinking of marrying her."

The student raises his eyebrows in disbelief.

"You know," Orlando said, carefully cutting the garlic cloves and putting the base of the food in the pan, "I have made a picture, I want to sell it in Italy, but I don't know how to name it. I provisionally named it 'Aphrodite's Island'," said the painter, pointing to the painting with a tomato in his hand.

"Wow!" the student smiled as he lit a cigarette, though his tongue was swollen with the effects of nicotine, approaching the face of the woman who was waiting on a pier with her feet in the water. "What a strange woman! Don't you have a magnifying glass? I would like to see her more closely."

"There's one in the drawer there. Have you noticed anything special? I painted it as a promise, as a woman waiting on the dock of an island, as a unique love, without which you cannot live, you know as in 'The French Lieutenant's Woman'. I don't know if you've read the novel. A woman waiting on the pier for a ship that is no longer coming, a lieutenant who may have forgotten how many women he loved in the ports where he threw the anchor. A modern Penelope."

"To me she looks like a woman who has just made love. She doesn't look like a woman who is waiting. Waiting tortures, you, it gives you a look like the mirror of a source of pain. The look of a woman who is waiting is like liquid boiling. This woman," said the student, bringing the magnifying glass to her face, "is like a flower that has met the sunlight; she is happy. The feeling is so intense that in a certain way the light curves around her as if the feeling is accompanying gravity. She seems to me like a woman who is listening to music or a woman who is already about to become a song. 'Aphrodite's Island' sounds like an advertisement for individually packaged cakes."

"Aphrodite is the ideal of beauty. Aphrodite on an island to escape to…"

"I like this painting," the student said, shaking his hand as if he were giving the speech away as a page. "It gathers the essentials of the avant-garde and the crisis at the same time. It looks like it's painted with a knife."

Surprised, Orlando approached the student and the picture with the steaming pan in his hand.

"I feel like in a Baudelaire poem. No, really… Baudelaire's woman throws the veil on the feminine ideal. Baudelaire retains Aphrodite's voluptuous body and lays a dog or hydra's head on her shoulders. If it were my painting, I would call it 'Dog Island', thinking of the woman who has just left me; anyway, she left me or not, she is the woman I'm interested in and who makes me miserable, therefore, in order to keep the exotic air of the atmosphere and to be worldwide at the same time, I would translate it into Spanish, which means that I could name this painting 'La Isla del Perro'."

Hearing the name of the painting, Orlando leaned back as if he had been hit. Looking at his own painting, it seemed to him for a moment that the colour spots were moving in the rhythms of a flamenco song, and the clouds around the pier pressed his heart. He felt the painted woman dancing.

"That's why I need you to name my paintings," the painter laughed, full of inspiration.

"How do you like the name?"

"There couldn't be a better one. But wait," Orlando said, wiping his fingers with a napkin. "I have to write it on the painting," and grabbing a brush, with a single move, wrote 'La Isla del Perro' as a signature in the corner of the canvas. Orlando's face suddenly flashed, and the student—watching his wet face of a blond teenager, with the curled millet on one side and long favourites, with his sharp nose drawn over a bright smile slipping to one side—realised that the painter had a ceramic-like face, with no wrinkles; a transparent face through which you could see your dreams as if you were watching the fish in an aquarium. Nothing expressed fatigue, the long drinking nights in restaurants, the parties and all the entertainment, his face untouched by emotion, only his eyes glowing as bright as lights, while the student turned purple with fatigue and amusement, his skin burning, becoming either red or orange.

"You know, for this title I could give you any picture in this room as a gift. Choose one."

"Never in my life have I received a single gift, except one from the University rector: a Mont Blanc pen. I have loved that pen. Only at the great Universities in the world, especially the American ones, there is the tradition that the eminent student will be given a pen as a gift. When that pen is given by your favourite teacher, it is especially precious. I once thought I had forgotten it in a club, and I searched the club for two hours with the owner of the club, who was my friend," said the student while smoking and posing in his underpants like a musician with his hand on a piano. "After searching and searching, as in an epic in which you have to go through the whole world to find the truth, I found it behind the car seat. I think I still have it at home, on my bookshelf. I haven't seen it for a long time, dear friend, so if you don't have a Mont-Blanc pen in the workshop, you can keep your paintings."

While eating spaghetti, the two friends got up from the table and watched the picture while chewing. To Orlando, the painting seemed much more beautiful now; with the name written at the bottom corner of the canvas, the painting was new, complete, intact, whole and well-done. That's why he hugged the student in a friendly way, but when the student turned to the rest of the spaghetti on his plate, he found himself in front of a man with some letters in his hands, looking at the two young men hugging in their underpants with a somewhat reproachful look. As if looking through the glass, he measured his son's new friend with his eyes. The student then looked down towards his own underwear, stained by the traces of his fingers anointed with spaghetti sauce, trying to hide the prominent shape of his limb highlighted by his elastic underwear. In order to somehow release the tension, the student instinctively reached out to Orlando's father, but as he squeezed the short-haired, grey whiskered man's hand, he felt the sauce on his fingers and wiped it with a napkin, realising he should have wiped his hand before, and that he shouldn't be shaking hands with an older man while only wearing underpants anyway. Instead of showing how intelligent he was through a discourse that expressed great erudition, the student grinned foolishly, explaining himself:

"I am a friend of Orlando's."

"He's my father," Orlando said smiling, after the man left scratching his head. "My parents live just opposite. We're on the same level, if you know what I mean."

"Your father!" exclaimed the student, pretending to be surprised. "I barely heard him enter. He found us hugging in our underwear," he said, slightly worried. "He may think…he may even think we are in some way together," he whispered bewildered.

"Don't worry," Orlando said calmly as if this was impossible. "He sees many things in my apartment. We communicate very well," said the painter looking at the clock and finishing the iron door. "A client is supposed to come, though. Put something on."

"I'm leaving anyway."

"Wait a minute, let me get some money from this guy. I haven't told you anything about Italy yet. Finish your coffee and you'll have time to leave." The student entered the bathroom and returned to the room looking for his clothes. Orlando's client was just leaving a pile of money on the table, analysing the door. Carefully packing it in special shock-resistant foils, he took his door and left without paying any attention to the student who slipped into the bedroom among paintings and sketches. When he was about to leave, Orlando stopped him, talking on the phone.

While the painter was talking on the phone, the student looked at the pile of money on the table. For him it was a small fortune and that was the moment when he understood that Orlando was spending impressive sums of money every night, even more than a millionaire who owned many luxury properties throughout the capital which he would rent to different embassies. The student brought his hand to his temple as if Orlando's gesture of calling the waiter twice, thrice, ten times in one night had hurt him, and all those raised hands, quickly unravelling in the student's mind, would surround the student like a tornado of hands, shattering the things touched in infinite particles, making him feel guilty.

"I must go home," insisted the student, slightly embarrassed.

"Wait a moment, I need to go to Iveşti, to get some money from some money lenders there."

"Iveşti?"

"It's very close, it's a train station, we take the short way. I can't drive, I've been drinking. Please," Orlando insisted, seeing that the student was hesitant.

"Money is not a problem," Orlando said, pointing to the pile of money on the table. "I beg you. We take the short way, around the iron and steel works."

"Let me tell you about Italy," Orlando said as they were heading to Iveşti. "I worked on a project in a bar in Bucharest. I am modest, I copied a painting by Rivera…"

"I don't know who Rivera is."

"Oh, he is a Mexican painter who has a proud name as long as a phrase. I can't possibly remember his full name…Diego María de la Concepción Juan Nepomuceno…anyway, he is known as Diego Rivera. He was married to Frida Kahlo."

"I have heard of Frida Kahlo."

"He has a painting that I particularly like, 'El Vendedora De Alcatraces'. A seller facing looking like an Aztec Indian on his knees under the burden of a sack or basket of tar, kind of water lilies, kind of sword lilies or aquatic plants. This Indian is wearing a crown on his head as if he was once a king, but his face expresses great humility as if he were an aristocrat, a prince, a last prince of the Aztecs humiliated to collect tar and sell it at the Spanish market in order to survive. I painted it on the wall of a bar in the old centre of Bucharest...I painted almost all the bars in the old centre...anyway, at the inauguration the owner comes with some guests among whom there was a guy who was good at art. Among them, there was also a former teacher of mine who introduced me to the art expert, a university professor at I do not know what art university in Italy. This guy looks at my painting tactfully and says something to the owner, but I couldn't hear the words very well, so I sat at the inaugurating table to see what he was thinking and at one point the guy told me the execution was good, but it is a fact that it was a copy. He would have expected the copy to be more daring."

"But I cannot aesthetically change the painting, I am modest, I am a craftsman," I say.

"He is the most talented student I have ever had, my former teacher confirmed, to defend me in a way, because this Italian guy spoke so self-sufficiently, with a show-off air and some sort of irritating superiority.

"He is really talented, the Italian said, but provincial...if he wants to be worldwide, he must exhibit on Brera District."

"Brera District?"

"Via Brera, Milan; Diego Rivera also exhibited there. When you exhibit the first painting, if you ever exhibit there, only then will you be an artist, and an artist by definition is worldwide, he can exhibit anywhere on the planet even when making a copy. I have been thinking of Brera District ever since I came from Bucharest. That Italian guy spoke to me with a superiority that was hard to bear. Okay, maybe I'm subjective. He seemed to be knowledgeable, but very stiff-necked and self-confident. I would like to exhibit there," Orlando said, while the student could barely reverse on a dark street. He turned the radio down to better focus on driving.

"I think we have a flat tyre," said the student worried.

"Oh, but we have almost reached the place, it's just around the corner. We could leave the car here."

"How do we do something like this?" the student said frightened, trying to break through the darkness of that place that made things worse, dissolving them.

Orlando pulled the wheel out of the trunk and opened a folding jack. Looking at the jack with no confidence, the student thought of mechanical pencil sharpeners and began to laugh.

"This is what you want to lift the car with?"

"Yeah, I have had flat tyres before. The jack works."

After the two of them changed the tyre, the student realised that it was a bit late, and it was more than likely that he would not arrive home that night, thinking he'd better call his mother, but when he searched for his phone, he realised there was no signal. Not even Orlando's mobile phone had signal. Looking closely at the narrow street like a road in the woods, the student thought it would be better to return. But just around the corner, the street suddenly lit up, although there was no street lamp.

"What might that be?" the student wondered in amazement as he looked at the colourful houses shining in the moonlight, with their roofs covered in brass, mirrors, and gilt in gold and silver foil.

"Have you never been to Iveşti? These are the gypsy castles in Iveşti. The clans here have become rich trading iron and plate from the iron and steel works in town. Let me talk. It won't take too long. We take the money and leave. Make sure you don't laugh," Orlando said cautiously as he entered the courtyard of a house full of gypsies sitting around smoking grills.

Orlando greeted everyone in turn and the student did the same but he then sank on a couch next to a huge marble staircase that went down in the shape of an upstairs arm, spreading its immaculate fingers on a black marble floor. Involuntarily turning his head on his back, the student stared at the ceiling full of plump angels and smiling, he remembered that he had seen that painting somewhere else…

"I talked to Sandokan earlier on the phone. We won't stay long. He is my friend and he is a writer. We came to take the money and leave."

"But you have to stay and taste some lamb," said a gentle and sweet Bulibaşa, swaying his multi-layered belly.

"You should also try my wine," the head of the clan lured him, grinning and flashing two gold teeth.

The student moved the glass aside, explaining that he was the driver, but the gypsy who had given it firmly tightened his arm and the student quickly grabbed the wine to avoid spilling it on his shirt. The wine was very hard and fragrant.

"This is monastery wine, it's good to drink in huge amounts, not by glass," Bulibaşa said. "I got it from Tudor Vladimirescu monastery. I mended their roof with sheet metal. But how much money should he give you?"

37

"Well not too much, €700."

"He's gone to cut off someone's hand because he didn't pay him the interest money for three months."

The student burst into laughter while putting the glass on a table so as not to spill the wine. He wiped his mouth with a napkin. There was a sudden silence in the room. The student found himself surrounded by an amphitheatre of faces through which an electric shock seemed to have passed.

Alarmed, Orlando stared at him and his friend suddenly started sweating, remembering that he wasn't allowed to laugh.

"But what does your friend write, letters to his girlfriends?"

"He writes what he can," Orlando said, looking at his watch. "It's late. If you want to give me that money, fine, if not, I can come some other time. It's no rush."

"Give him €200 until Sandokan comes, to calm him down," Bulibaşa said to an older gypsy guy who searched his pockets and gave the painter two €50 banknotes. "Be patient, Orlando, Sandokan is coming soon. He gives you the other 500. Did you also make that painting with Tarzan in Stăneşti, at the border of the village?"

"Yes," Orlando answered with no sign of nervousness.

"I liked it a lot, there is a hidden message in it. You can see the jungle, lions, elephants, monkeys, Tarzan…"

"They gave me a picture from the Jungle Book. I paint what my client asks me to paint…"

"Yes, here," Bulibaşa said, pointing his chin towards the ceiling, "I don't know what Sandokan meant, but all I can see is just some plump angels, as fat as if they were raised together with the pigs."

"Do you happen to understand anything?" said Bulibaşa to his wife who went down with their little boys and girls. One of the girls started to look at the student, who covered his face with his glass quenching his thirsty, as he recognised the girl in the colourful skirt who had slipped over her ass in the bar. Worried, he wanted to ask about the toilet, but Orlando, anticipating what he was going to ask, whispered between his teeth.

"Relax, they don't have an in-house toilet. It's in the yard. For them it's an offense to have a toilet in the house."

"Sandokan wanted me to paint the Sistine Chapel for him and the Sistine Chapel is what I did," Orlando said loudly to Bulibaşa, shrugging his shoulders. "That's how he saw it in Italy. Nobody else has such a thing, it is a painting by Michelangelo Buonarotti, 'La Nuevo Luce Della Cappella Sistina'. That's how he saw it in Italy, that's what he wanted, that's what I did. He gave me the pictures and I painted what was in the photos."

"Yes, I know, Sandokan is well-travelled. If that's what he wanted…I'd rather have wanted Tarzan on the walls, an elephant, a monkey and that was all. If that's what he wanted, he also told me that there is a church in Italy painted with plump angels that the rich from all over the world admire. If this is what the world admires, that's fine."

"I paint what the client asks me to," Orlando said, flashing his eyes and the student understood that the painter had already drunk too much. Intimidated, he put the cup of wine on the table, realizing that he had just drank a whole glass of wine; with so many cups and glasses on the table, he no longer knew whether he drank from the cup he was supposed to or if he drank from the cup belonging to Bulibasa.

"Look, here comes Sandokan," Bulibaşa breathed in with relief.

Sandokan entered the house and left the sword to a boy who placed it in its place on a Japanese stand after he wiped it with a piece of white silk.

"Sandokan, Orlando came to take the money for the painting."

Sandokan lit a cigarette and tossed back a glass of wine, looking at the freshly painted ceiling, with his hat on his sweaty neck.

"How much money do I owe you, Orlando?"

"What we agreed. I have just received €100 and I need another 600."

"Give him the money after he has finished," Bulibaşa said.

"Well, I'm done," Orlando said with a serious look.

"Well, Orlando, I know you're a friend of Maricel Ivan, but you don't fool me," Bulibasa said and the room got all frozen. "Where are the angels' feet, can you show me?"

"This is the painting; the angels have no legs. They have wings," Orlando said with an innocent voice.

"Do they have wings and hands and they do not have legs?" Bulibaşa said, more and more nervous.

"This is Michelangelo's painting."

"Who the fuck is Mikellangolo? Well, everyone knows angels are pink, you painted them almost transparent blue. They have hands but no legs."

"But…this is how the painting looks," Orlando shrugs his shoulders.

"Look, Dad," said a girl pointing to the student, "this one hit me over the pussy last night…"

"Who?" Bulibaşa asked, turning to the student, smirking like an armoured car. "Give me the sword to cut off his head! Wait, I'll cut it off with the axe," Bulibaşa yelled, lifting an axe from the table and throwing it to the student who dodged it, the axe flying like a tomahawk stabbing into the railing of the marble staircase that was actually made of plaster. The gypsies jumped over the two, but in the ambush of punches and legs, they somehow managed to escape to the stairs and Orlando dragged the student after him towards some scaffolding. They jumped to the roof and slid on the roof tiles in the street, the student feeling how the mirrors on the roof were tearing chunks from his back as if he had slipped on a barbed wire gutter. From the street, since the gypsies were coming from all over armed with droppings and axes, they hurried to the forest gasping, but after a few meters, they slipped into a ravine and found themselves almost swimming in a swamp. When they got out of the water, they saw the gypsies looking for them among the bushes with their lanterns and hid in an empty tank in a shed. As they were trying to get out of the tank, its lid opened and a stream of water flew in, almost suffocating them. Panicked, the student wanted to shout for help by waving his hands, but he felt the bottom of the tank and became calmer. Then the tank started to move, jumping over some holes.

The student seemed to hear Russian voices. His heart was pounding in his ears. When the tank finally stopped and it was quiet, they removed the lid of the tank and jumped into a garden. A dog burst out, barking at their feet, and lights lit up throughout the length of a barbed wire fence. Orlando pulled the student towards him just as a burst of machine gun was heard, then a call followed and the two of them found themselves in the bright light of a spotlight, frightened by the fear of the bullets that had whispered by their ears. Orlando turned with his hands raised. The student wanted to turn too, but a soldier's boot pressed on his hand. The soldier twisted his hands behind his back and put handcuffs on.

The student woke up in a dark room on a wide damp board that was supposedly a bed. Getting accustomed to the darkness, he saw a line of crouching prisoners leaning against a wall and smoking.

"Where have you put the cigarettes?" asked a prisoner with a crooked nose, who had hitherto sat in the shade but at an arm's distance, camouflaged in the shadow of the wall.

"What cigarettes?"

"They are not playing games," the prisoner warned in a whispering voice. "Your comrade is being questioned."

"I have no idea where we are," said the student, completely confused.

The prisoner started laughing.

"You don't know where you are? You'll soon find out," said the young man with a Moldovan accent.

Suddenly Orlando arrived with his eyes flashing like electric fireflies, crouching next to the student. Seeing his swollen nose, the student burst into tears, remembering his college mate climbing down the stairs on the cliff, asking if he was hanging out with Orlando.

"They'll ask you about cigarettes," Orlando said.

"What cigarettes?" the student trembled.

"This is a Russian border guard unit specialised in cigarette smuggling," Orlando whispered. "It's best not to contradict them. You have to agree to them, otherwise it's getting complicated. In this country, only the illegal crossing of the border is punishable by 6 years imprisonment."

"Six years in prison?" the student said panicked. "But I did nothing wrong!"

"You better tell the truth," the prisoner said, giving Orlando a cigarette, but Orlando politely refused. The student, however, lit one, shaking and with tears in his eyes, remembering that he had not seen his family for a few days, and that his family knew absolutely nothing about him; they must be very worried or they may have even signalled his disappearance. Suddenly, the student hit the concrete wall with his head. The blow shook the room like an earthquake. A few prisoners barely managed to calm him down.

"Did they at least allow you to call home?" the student asked with a lost look, trickling himself along the wall after the crisis.

"If they had allowed me to call, I wouldn't have called home. I would have called Maricel Ivan."

While waiting for the interrogation, the student's face changed colours, becoming purple and then yellow, like a lemon, with his eyes sunk into his head and barely flickering. At one point, the door of the room opened and the Romanians were pushed down a corridor with barred stairs. The guards covered their heads with pillows. Walking along the corridors, Orlando felt the rotten heat of overcrowded dormitories, seeing with his mind's eyes the bunk beds with two inmates sleeping in each bed.

We are in a prison, thought the student. *Poor me!*

The guards removed the pillows over their heads in front of an office. Trembling, the student tried to move his hands which were locked in a plastic collar. A guard cut off his collar with a knife and only then did the student see the prisoner dressed in uniform, smiling and holding out a cigarette. The student lit the cigarette, almost hypnotised, but Orlando politely refused again.

"Here you are your personal belongings. Check them. Is it fine?"

"That's fine," Orlando said, checking his jeans pocket.

"You had to tell me from the beginning that you were Maricel Ivan's friends. You have a vodka box here."

"Who can I say the vodka is from?"

"He knows. You are free to go."

When they arrived at the border in a bus full of potatoes, they waited in the customs office to have their documents checked. Surprisingly, although they had no documents, they were allowed to take the tram to the city and no one asked them about the box of vodka.

A few days later, the student was making coffee in the kitchen, completely undecided, his movements slow; the slower he moved, the more he seemed to enjoy life by walking on a song that only the inspired ones can hear in the murmur of things. He had been sleeping next to his sick mother who couldn't get out of bed. He had held her in his arms all night, watching her sleep. The coffee refreshed his body like a gust of wind wandering a deserted city. He heard a knock and went slowly, really slowly, to open the door.

"I'm going to Italy to sell 'Dog Island' on Via Brera," Orlando told him, elfishly smiling in the frame of the door, wearing a fragrant raw silk shirt, as immaculate as a snowdrop. "Are you coming with me? We'll have to sell paintings to survive. If needed, we'll sleep in the car. But I think that won't be the case. Sandokan apologised and sent you a gift as a writer."

The student grabbed a small box packed in glossy paper and without opening it he felt like it was a Mont Blanc pen kit. He felt his logo under his finger. He smiled as he stared out of the window with a look like a sword. The unnaturally close sky had a heavy colour, almost thrown on a canvas with a knife.

"I'm not driving at night, I want to make this clear!" the student said, raising his right hand to his temple so there was no confusion.

La Cigarétte Apres L'Amour

There was a knock on the door. The poet startled, tiptoeing to the window as if he were climbing a trench. There was a man in the dark street. He was standing like a pillar in a cemetery, deserted and threatening. The poet drew a telescopic sight to his eye, but he could barely distinguish part of his face. "An Arab," the poet thought, feeling himself hunted by a paid assassin. It was drizzling and cold outside. He could hear a cough and the figure moving. There was such peace on the boulevard that the poet could feel the cough like a firearm and he dropped the telescopic sight on the decayed floor. Feeling about, he reached the window. "Shit," he said, realizing he'd moved the curtain.

The figure struck a lighter and lit a cigarette. Looking up at the tall tower-like house, Charles felt as if someone was throwing a spear from that place. The poet could barely see his face, but when the figure put his lighter into his pocket, for a moment he could see his worn-out, water-soaked shoes.

The poet lit a candle, cautiously descending the stairs. He carefully opened the door, exiting onto the boulevard.

"Sir," he said to the figure, "you have been standing in the street for more than two hours. What do you want from me? How much do I owe you?"

Charles dropped his cigarette from his mouth in astonishment. He had almost fallen asleep, trembling beneath the sharp drizzle.

"I, sir, am looking for…writer Vaucaire, sir, Michel Vaucaire, the poet," Charles said, stammering.

"And who are you, may I ask?"

"I…" began Charles, intimidated, "I'm a…trumpeter."

"A trumpeter," the poet smiled after a few serious moments. "How interesting! I thought you were a debt collector."

"No, sir, I'm a composer. I got references from Voltaire. I was told you lived near Invalides on number 9 Jose Maria de Hérédia. That's how I got here," said Charles, barely breathing and refraining from coughing.

"Come inside the house quickly," said the poet trembling while looking at the old chestnut trees on the boulevard, sizzling in the cold as if they were trying to cover each other, as if they were sighing or sobbing.

"Beware of your steps! The yard is full of old things and the owner lives next door; should he hear us, we're finished."

"Take off your overcoat. Put it on the hanger here," Michel said, lighting another candlestick and putting the telescopic sight under a rifle on the wall.

"I thought you had a bat in your hand."

"It's a telescopic sight. I use it to watch the people in the street. I sometimes like to see people from a distance. People, sir, are cannibals. I got this gun from my dad. He fought in Verdun. Arthur Vocaire. That was my father's name. We will light a fire," said the poet, heading to the library.

"Tell me you don't want to set the books on fire," Charles said with a frightened voice, when the poet turned with an arm of incunabula.

"Sir, I ran out of wood three months ago. I'm a poet. Nobody gives a penny for poetry. That's why I give piano lessons," said the poet, putting another lit candle on the piano.

"Alas, but this is a Bäsendorfer. It's a treasure," said Charles, sitting on the stool and trying the piano delicately. "Oh, wait for two seconds…" Charles opened the piano and tuned it, correcting a false note and putting the piano key in his pocket so as not to forget it.

"You said you were a trumpeter."

"I'm a composer. I compose my piano songs. I'm desperate. A few years ago, I decided to compose in order to earn my living. I couldn't sell anything, not even a sound. Dad used to ask me what I was going to become when I grew up. I used to answer him I wanted to be a trumpeter."

"I used to tell my father I wanted to be an astronaut living in the clouds."

"But what's that you are doing?"

"I'm going to burn some older T-shirts. I would burn some of the carpet, but it's not mine and it's a bit damp."

"We could burn my shoes… I feel like I'm walking barefoot anyway."

"No, no way," Michel said, no shoes. "In the meantime, the coffee is ready."

"Wait a minute, do you really want to burn this book? It is the 'Legend of the Centuries' by Victor Hugo. I have been meaning to read this book for a long time! It's a rarity even in public libraries. However, you can only consult it at the reading room."

"But it's in lyrics and it's almost mouldy. I'd give it to you to read, but it's as if I'd sentenced you to death. You risk being poisoned when turning its pages. You need to wet your fingers well. I also have this book— 'Complete Works by Shakespeare'. Shall we burn Hugo or incinerate Shakespeare? Which one do you prefer?"

"Better Shakespeare, he is not French."

"That's right. It's exactly what I thought. I am Swiss by origin but I have been speaking French since I was born. If you don't mind, while you were waiting in the street, I saw that you were smoking."

"Would you like a cigarette?"

"Would I like one? I haven't smoked a real cigarette in more than three months. I don't know what others are like, sir, but when I smoke a cigarette, I feel like a prince, like a man, sir, enjoying his spare time."

"So," Michel said, almost dizzy, inhaling lingeringly from his cigarette. "How can I help you?"

"Sir, do you believe in God?"

"Do I believe in God? As most people, I only believe in God when I need Him. There are many times when I doubt that God has ever existed or that He may even exist, but since I was born, I have never doubted, I have not doubted poetry for a single moment.

"Physics taught me how the universe started, how planets were formed, but no one knows how beings appeared. The human being, sir, I'm sure of it, started with poetry. Poetry is the fourth dimension in the universe, the one that gives meaning to it. Without poetry, living makes no sense. Without poetry, the universe is empty, absurd, chaotic and meaningless. When I came to Paris, I was young. I was 19 years old. A gypsy woman read my hand and told me that a song was going to change my life, a single song. I remember her words."

"When you have created this song, you will walk on the street as if you stepped on precious stones."

"Did you tell her beforehand that you were a musician?"

"Yes."

"Of course, she told you that," said the poet, following a roll of smoke with his eyes.

"Now, sir," Charles finally said, "I have this feeling that I have written the music, but I need the lyrics. I don't know how to write the lyrics. I'm not a poet. I only know about ta-ta-ta... My song has no words; as you said, it is empty, absurd and meaningless; it's like clapping with one hand only. But my song is there, I feel it, I have it here," Charles said with a bright look in his eyes, waving some older scores.

"If I like the song, I will definitely write the lyrics, but I, sir," Michel said, lighting another cigarette and feeling a rush of nausea at the same time, waiting for it to pass. "I have a condition."

"Which one?"

"I also need a song, the song of my existence. This song should be called 'La cigarétte Apres L'amour'. I have a theory about smoking, sir. It is impossible that before the industrial revolution everyone smoked en masse. It must have been only the chiefs, only the princes, only the kings who used to smoke. 'La Cigarette Apres L'amour' is the very moment of happiness, the moment when you realise that you are happy and that you have been burned by the lust of love, sir. It's the moment subsequent to making love, sir. Smoking a cigarette after making love is happiness itself. There are many women in my memory, but it is only one, but one, who has fulfilled me. It was incredible!

"While in bed, she used to turn into a fabulous animal, she was like a centaur. After she had devoured her love, she lit a cigarette at the window, in contre-jour, and her face of a fabulous animal gradually changed. She slowly took her real face and age and turned back to reality, which means that everything she lived in bed, all our love, brought her closer to dream, madness and delirium, in any case to a much more intense reality, to some sort of surreal existence, if I can express myself this way, closer to the heart of reality. If you can transpose into music my theory on the cigarette after love, I, sir, at any time, at absolutely any time, I will be at your disposal with my lyrics, as long as I live, remember this," said the poet raising a finger to draw attention on what he was saying.

"I already have this song. I think I've already written it."

"Perfect. Let's hear the song of your life, then. The song for which you expect my lyrics."

"Let's hear it."

Charles placed his scores on the stand. He put on his glasses and started to sing. After the first musical phrase, Michel sipped his coffee as if he were surprised by an unexpectedly good taste. The chickpea coffee in the pot was horrible, but the music was incredible. He stood and listened intently. The notes sounded serious, as important as if they were being heard in a cathedral.

"I have written it for an orchestra…" Charles explained himself as if in apology, but Michel made a sign with his hand as if he was telling him to forget about the explanations and continue playing. Suddenly, he had the urge to dance, as if he were listening to a waltz. When the song was over, Charles sadly turned the lid over the piano, looking at how the flames devoured a torn blouse as well as Hugo's book…'The Legend of the Centuries'. The book was crackling with flames and the pages turning black with heat. Michel looked at his numb arms. He had goose bumps. He was going to say something, but the gate could be heard banging.

"Have you just started a fire, poet?! Do you throw parties at midnight? Do you allow yourself to play the piano and bring women in the middle of the night, when you haven't paid your rent for three months?"

"I'll pay you, Monsieur Blanchet. Do not panic. I'll pay you back soon," Michel said, calmly showing Charles the way to the back door.

While doing so, he whispered to him:

"Leave me your sheets. Next week I will come to the cafe, to Voltaire, with the lyrics. I'll set up an appointment with a woman singer. I always expect you to come to me. Come in during the day for a coffee."

"I have a feeling that all my past was burned in the fire in your room, my dear friend," Charles whispered to him before going out onto the boulevard. "I will remember that you burned your books to make me a coffee."

"Don't worry, I have already started writing the lyrics. It's a wonderful song. I already know what it's going to be called."

"What?" asked Charles, trembling with curiosity.

"Je ne regrette rien," Vaucaire whispered, looking backwards to see if the owner had sensed his presence.

"But this is not an appropriate title for a song," said Dumont disappointedly. "'Je ne reggrette rien' is like saying 'je m'en fous'."

"Exactly," Michel laughed and tried to explain a little more, but he made a sign with his hand. "Wait for the lyrics, please."

When he reached the first intersection, Charles stopped and listened to the owner's hysterical cries. They could be heard so clearly:

"You'd better give me the money, unless you want me to come with the doormen tomorrow and jump your piano. You're going to go to the debtors' prison, Vocaire. Pay your rent or take your scraps and get lost. The cafes are full of tramps."

Stylishly dressed in the latest London fashion, with a jacket and sports shoes, Michel Vocaire walked into Voltaire café after a week, greeting the bartender and his friends, but the bartender looked away instead of answering his greeting.

"Coffee," Vocaire said confidently, because he had a few francs in his pocket.

"Forgive me, Mr Vocaire, but we don't go on tick today."

Michel gritted his teeth because he had just seen an ineffable blonde in the cafe, a new face who was likely to be an Arts student.

"I pay in advance, you may keep the change," Michel said, dropping two coins from his fingers.

"I could pass it into the debit of your account, if you wish," said the bartender cautiously.

"Maurice, we have known each other for seven years, you should make me a statue and place it in your cafe, if we think of how much money I spend on the parties. Please bring me a coffee, tomorrow I'll pay your full debt. Do not panic. Just wait until tomorrow."

"I look forward to seeing that," the bartender muttered under his breath.

"How beautiful the Seine looks today, as smooth as an ocean, as calm as marble," said the poet looking at the quiet river which seemed like a shining sword resting on the knees of a musketeer. "I'm looking for composer Charles Dumont," said the poet with a loud voice suddenly, so that everyone could hear him.

"I don't know him," the bartender shrugged. "I don't know who he is."

"How's that? He's a musician, an artist. He asked for references about me in this place. Nobody knows him?"

The customers at the back, where the blonde woman was, also nodded.

"Where's Antoine, she knows everyone. He's a short guy, he has an Arabic face. He is wearing a stained brown overcoat."

"Oh, I know him," said a newspaper seller. "He left Paris. I saw him in the morning at Gare du Nord, looking for a train. He has a brother at Clermond Ferrand, but he didn't have all the money."

The poet ran into the street after a taxi. The bartender carefully set the coins aside, peering at the coffee steaming on the counter.

Passing through the crowd in the train station, the poet turned to the ticket offices, looking at the platforms at the same time. He found Charles on a bench, counting some coins in a handkerchief.

"My dear friend," said the poet, hugging him. "I have the lyrics."

"What's the point of having them?" Charles said quietly. "I no longer have a home. The porters threw me into the street. I haven't paid rent for five months. I could barely get my clothes I am wearing. I'm leaving, dear friend, to Spain. I have a brother in Figures, if he agrees to have me. If his wife allows."

"Alas, no, I have the lyrics."

"What title did you give to my song?"

"I regret nothing."

"But I told you this is not a good song title," Charles said disappointedly, looking after the trains. "It resembles ordinary speech. I regret nothing, I do not care at all."

"Exactly, but you have to listen to it. I have already set up an appointment with a woman singer."

"Who?"

"Edith Piaf."

"But I've been to Edith Piaf twice. She didn't like the song. Oh, there's no point in doing this. And anyway, Edith Piaf only sings the well-known composers' songs. Let me go."

"On no account. In no way. You're coming with me. We've run out of time."

"And will Edith Piaf come to your attic?" Charles asked incredulously when he was already in the taxi.

"Absolutely, I have known Edith since she was a kid. I've taken her to the Jesuits school countless times. She always keeps her word, especially when asked by Michel Vaucaire. At 1 pm sharp she will be at my place and listen to your song on my lyrics."

"Who, Madame Edith Piaf?" the taxi driver asked without turning back. "No way, Madame Piaf is in Versailles with President Charles de Gaulle. He gives her a medal and makes her a UNESCO French ambassador."

"She will be there," said Michel, gritting his teeth, slapping Charles on his shoulders, not too sure of himself. "You will see, she will come!"

When they reached Jose Maria de Hérédia Boulevard, Michel was surprised to see the owner's porter carrying his piano on the stairs. The courtyard was full of mouth-watering crowds. Everything was carefully carried in boxes and bags placed directly on the ground. The porters were working hard, as if they had unloaded a caravan. Suddenly someone was heard loading a weapon. The court got stoned.

"I'm Michel Vaucaire, the owner of this piano. I will shoot without a warning. At the first innocent move, I'll turn you into angels. Take the piano to the attic now." The crouched porters looked at the owner. Gasping in fear and anger, he backed down, looking at the gun.

The poet looked into his eyes.

"You will receive the money for the rent today. Take my piano back. Hurry up!" Vaucaire grumbled in a loud voice and the porters made their way back.

"Mr Michel Vaucaire?" he heard someone asking him from behind and when a security colonel returned, he took his weapon from his hands.

"Are you allowed to carry this carbine?"

"It belonged to my father. He fought in the First World War. Back then, the soldiers were allowed to come back home with their weapons. Who are you?"

"Gerard Mouron, colonel of guard and protection of the republican guard. The president will arrive in a few moments with Edith Piaf. The lady has an appointment with you at 1pm. Ah, here comes the convoy. This weapon stays with me."

The limousine convoy occupied almost the entire boulevard, which was eventually closed for security reasons. The officers in uniform and in civilian clothing occupied their positions in the yard. General de Gaulle was carefully arming Edith Piaf, followed by a group of RFI reporters and a live television car.

"The President of France," said the general in a gallant voice, heading to the cameraman with his back to the crowd of idlers, "is at Mrs Eidth Piaf's disposal, the most important ambassador of France."

"The business card of France today is this voice—the voice of Edith Piaf. Were you saying, lady, that you had an appointment with a poet who wanted to propose a song to you?" The tall general was trying to see above the people. Among the crowd of idlers, there was the president speaking to himself, because Edith was too short and the disease had made her even shorter. The world stepped aside and Edith Piaf, accompanied by the president, entered a house which had been emptied of everything, with its windows wide open, without curtains, and in the middle of the room there waited a piano.

"Dear Edith," said Vocaire, "Mr President…dear Edith, I am so glad you came," said Vocaire excitedly, with his arms wide open before the flashes of the cameras. "I want to introduce you to composer Charles Dumont."

"I have a feeling that we do know each other," said Edith, reaching out her hand, but either due to emotion or fatigue,

Charles stood still, tilting his head slightly. Edith withdrew her hand with a slight pirouette so that the photographs would have a favourable angle. By the time he realised it, it was too late for Charles. Edith had turned her back.

"Let's hear the song, gentlemen," Edith said in a crystalline voice. "Let's not make the President of France wait."

Charles sat on the stool before the scores. He breathed in, with his face lit by flashes. With a smile, Vaucaire settled the texts on the staves, but Charles remained motionless.

"I don't have my glasses," whispered Vaucaire in his ear in a state of shock. "I don't know where I left them."

"Stay calm, please, I'll sing."

"Unfortunately, the composer does not have the glasses on him," said the poet, "but I will sing, if you bear me. I know the lyrics by heart. I myself have written them."

The assistance vibrated amused and curious responses. The flashes were arrested on the faces of the two.

"The song is called 'Je ne regrette rien'. Master, give me a G clef."

"Yes," said Michel, clearing up his voice, taking a tenor posture, resting his left fingers on the piano and bringing his right palm to his chest.

Charles closed his eyes, leaving his fingers free on the keyboard as if he had let loose some ogres in a meadow in search of their prey. His fingers gently touched the keyboard and the room filled with ample sounds, as if an entire orchestra were playing.

A TV5 car started broadcasting the song live. The presenter turned to the window looking at the TV car in the street and received the transmission confirmation from the sound engineer. Michel began to sing calmly as if it were a piano lesson. In order not to be intimidated by the crowd in the room, he closed his eyes. His voice raised clear and rested like a bird awakened by the first ray of the sun.

"No, I do not regret anything, neither the good that was done to me, nor the evil, everything is equal to me…no, I do not regret anything, no, I do not regret anything…"

When the song was over, Michel opened his eyes for assistance. It seemed that the still room was slightly overturned to one side, losing its gravity.

Edith stood still, astonished as if she had received a bullet in her chest. She was barely breathing—the flashes were slipping on her astonished face; a shocked face that had just darkened. There was a heavy silence like a slab.

"Ah, this is the song of my life," said the singer clearly. "I feel like I'm living again. I want to sing it right now. Master, please."

Waiting for a reaction, Charles could no longer lift his hands from his knees and started to cry. But as he tried to control his tears, they burst even louder as if from a shaking geyser. Michel leaned towards him as if he wanted to protect him.

"Dear friend, please…"

Feeling his emotion, Edith reached over and touched his shoulders, but the touch turned into a hug and Charles started to say in tears:

"Please, forgive me."

"Master Dumont," said Edith with kindness, "please, I want to sing this song."

Weeping a little quieter, Charles started the song, waiting for the singer's voice to take over. His hands trembled on the keyboard almost instantly. When he found the piano's melodic line, her voice rose as if opening the windows, across the boulevard that was listening transfixed, and that was the moment when Charles realised that the song had incredible, untranslatable lyrics, of an unearthly beauty, especially because they were sung by Edith Piaf in French, only in French and in no other language. In France, watches stopped when Edith Piaf sang 'Je ne regrette rien' for the first time. When the clapping of applause started in Michel Vocaire's attic, Charles with a tear-streaked face felt a gust of wind lift his hair on his forehead, and the piano vibrated as deep as a launched ship on its maiden voyage.

Life as a Gunshot

Two silhouettes suddenly emerged from the blazing building, but they were barely distinguishable and appeared to be just two spots in the fiery background. He saw them leaning away from the flames and pointed to them, but no one saw them.

A flaming balcony and part of the hotel's front collapsed over a fire brigade vehicle, almost destroying it. As if catapulted, a piece of the aluminium folding ladder fluttered into a van, turning it upside down. The policemen belonging to the special intervention troops were trying to get out of the van. They could barely handle the straps of the automatic weapons that caught them under like a fishing net. Police vehicles were coming from all over the place as if the hotel was besieged. The lights and sirens seemed to fuel the fire that suddenly became unexpectedly powerful, threatening the entire old neighbourhood. The air was full of sparks that threateningly sounded like tracers. The wind from the Mediterranean turned them into missiles. The first victims of the fire were already lying on the ground, their faces burnt. Everyone trying to get out of the hotel was restrained, legitimised, controlled, held with their hands raised and facing the walls of the neighbouring buildings. A policeman pushed a fire fighter who had dropped his helmet on the ground, thinking he was a suspect. Trying to get back to his colleagues, he reached out his hands to avoid any possible obstacle.

The silhouettes of the people running away did not seem real. They were rising as if they were kites. But the American followed them. At the corner of the hotel, he discovered the cobbled medieval alley, narrow as a rescue path leading to the old port. While stumbling onto the ground because of the irregular stones, the old walls built hundreds of years ago by the first Templars when they disembarked from the sea pushed him forward slightly, preventing him from falling. The street whirred like a sword on a warrior's knees. The American ran feeling himself pushed forward by the rhythm of a battle song. Suddenly the neon lights of a beer banner flashed on the face of the first person running and the American gritted his teeth when he recognised him.

A shadow remained behind, preparing the ambush. A spark lit a stain of fuel on his trousers below his knees and Doyle smiled, remembering how he had entered the hotel with a can of diesel oil that he splashed on the halls, explaining in English to the receptionist that he was ridding the house of rats and that all rats must be exterminated. The receptionist did not understand anything anyway. While he was trying to talk on the phone to the landlord, the flames had already engulfed the corridors in thick, dark smoke. Bending to extinguish the flame on his trousers, he could hear how the shot made the windows rumble. The bullet whistled passing his ear, curled into a gargoyle and rolled over the cobblestoned street.

You paid assassin, Doyle thought while smiling and didn't stop running. *Fellow, with such a weapon, it's hard to shoot while running.* The runaway fired backward once again without aiming and he started running as well, heading for the harbour. He suddenly felt a kick in his ankles. He flipped over some dumpsters and when he tried to look back, the sharp edge of the sidewalk almost cut his leg. Jumping over it, the American kicked the gun into a trash can.

The American suddenly dodged, getting into some heavy traffic. The light of the boulevard almost blinded him. Confused, he looked to both sides and caught sight of him just as he was closing the door of a car. The car started gasping like a kicked hyena. He almost jumped in the middle of the traffic. "Shit…fucking hell, bloody crazy shit, shit of the shit," Doyle screamed, continuing to run after the car that was disappearing in the traffic. The American was running haphazardly while swearing. Looking at a motorcyclist, he managed to catch sight of a plaque naming 'La Canebiere Street'. *Shitty language*, he thought to himself, trying to pronounce the word. When he reached the top of the hill near a traffic light, he breathed in looking over the boulevard. He saw the car quickly sliding just near the Old Port. Looking ahead, he took a deep breath and continued to run among the cars. He remembered his boss before sending him to Marseille; when he entered the office, his boss was just making the recommendations. "Who, Popeye? Popeye has a greyhound nose. Those greyhounds hunting the mobster.

"In fact, it is only Doyle that can recognise him. When Popeye smells him out, he finds him in a snake hole. He raises his nose in the wind and it's over."

I hope you're right, boss, Doyle thought, jumping forward.

Charnier waited at a traffic light and when it turned green, he started. He suddenly pushed the brake, almost touching the car in front of him. He sounded the horn nervously. He climbed down. There was a wall of cars ahead. Suddenly, when he turned, he saw the American throwing his overcoat that prevented his escape. *You should have killed him*, thought the Frenchman, hitting the hood. He dropped his gloves and abandoned his car, going out of sight by the corner. When Doyle arrived around the corner of the building, an overcrowded market full of tourists completely confused him. He looked in all directions. An annoyed old woman was watching him. The pigeons she was feeding suddenly flew to the roof of the opera house. The tall man with the small hat, worn more like a cap, suddenly looked to his left and right, back and forth, as if he were delivering boxing hits. A pancreatic seizure hit him on his right side, almost knocking him down like a knock-out shot in his liver, performed by a professional boxer. As he lifted his trunk, he saw Charnier's gaze flashing in a watch window. Turning, he saw the tram crammed with people heading for the old port. As if he was looking through a telescopic sight, he saw his hat for a moment before losing himself among the crowd. But it was more of an opinion, for a fraction of a second. The American breathed in. He looked at the traffic and he started to follow the tram. He knew he was there. He shook his right leg trying to escape the pain around his liver. He wanted to stop a car by showing them the policemen badge, but he continued to run in a disorderly manner, trying to save his last powers. He squeezed his chewing gum hard, his tooth almost giving in under such pressure. He suddenly saw the tram stopped near the docks. The crowd started to get off. With his hand on his stomach, he entered a market that led to a utility garage. On the left there were the warehouses with rows of huge trucks waiting to be loaded. To the right—there was the deserted entrance to the docks district. The ghetto, whiffing of urine, steadily smoked in the midday sun. The harbour slaves were at work. When he turned back, he looked at the harbour in confusion while a yacht was disappearing around the harbourmaster's building. He caught a glimpse of him coming down below the deck, resting his hands on the narrow railings. But it might very well not have been him. It was just a snap of a moment. The yacht moved on silently. The American was almost oozing on the fences near the docks. A fighting dog tossed him near an unfinished wall. He looked to the yacht in the corner of his eye. He climbed over some garbage cans and stepped into a courtyard. The owner watched him in amazement while watering his garden. The yacht turned to the bay and he suddenly saw Charnier coming out from under the deck with a coffee in his hand, enjoying the magnificent Mediterranean landscape with its coasts full of tourists and its luxurious hotels, its scented gardens, guarded by the cliffs of the mountains so old they had collapsed into themselves in a solid fortress wall.

With a heavy breath, the American climbed up the dam near the old lighthouse, leaning against the wall with his back. He touched his boot with his hand and set aside the casing hook. He was under the impression that the gun was not there. Its pipe was half the length of a finger. He aimed at the yacht, waiting for it to get closer. The sun, right in front of him, mixed its shape and distance. Checking his weapon, he realised he was aiming too low. Then he lifted the gun, resting it on his palm above the yacht and lowering it calmly to the figure. He called out the name, uttering the word perfectly: "Charnier!" And he pulled the trigger. The shot confused the flight of a seagull flying high above. Hearing his name, Charnier turned to the old lighthouse, distinguishing a squatter by the stairs. He recognised the policeman's gaze and blinked at the shot, taking his hand to his chest to cover his wound. The yacht continued its silent passage through the ships of the port with its deserted deck. The American turned on his back, hawking. His spirits lifted in jubilation. He was sure he'd hit him in the heart. He smiled with his mouth wide open, biting the air.

The Book Seller

When the student's first book came out two years ago, his father, who was a builder, was returning from the iron and steel works with some newspapers under his arm, which were hiding the book, just like old peasants used to hold their money wrapped within their overcoat, and every time he met somebody he knew in the neighbourhood, he reached out his arm just like a wing and discreetly presented his son's book, which had been published under a pseudonym.

"I don't understand why you wrote using a penname. My name is Patraş Mitică, and you are Andrei Patraş, not Arthur Romanesco. What name is this? A half-breed name. I'm not a Romanesco, I'm a Patras descendant."

"Father, it is a French resonance pen name, as I have always wanted to study in Paris, at the Sorbonne University, and to live in the Latin Quarter, at the very core of the Vanguard," the student explained, blinking his blue eyes. His father pretended he was upset, but his imagination filled him with light. "And Arthur, Arthur is the king of the Knights of the Round Table," the student continued, spinning a yarn of happenings about the knights he so well knew, as if they were his very school mates and not the characters of old books that only a few people on the planet had read.

In the street, from a distance, the student had several times seen his father's gesture of raising his arm, the gesture of a Phoenix bird protecting a talisman or a treasure, but he was paying no attention to this episode. While the people were following him through the neighbourhood, from their balconies, from the corners of the block, from the back of the cars, just like elite shooters, the student did not realise this, living as a light-hearted guy, only concerned with his literary theories. He was unaware he had become a star in his neighbourhood, more likely a target. His father knew how to advertise him effectively.

"He wrote under a pseudonym because he had a contract with the Vanguard in Paris, which sponsored his studies. All universities in France are struggling to have him as their student," explained Pop Patraş, with his eyes full of light just like forest springs. "The French Academy, the highest cultural institution in France, has given him a distinction, a Round Table Knight's medal, which means that an academician armchair is already being prepared for him."

"This is impossible," the people in the neighbourhood used to tell him, visibly impressed and bewildered by such news, especially because after showing them the newspaper articles reviewing his son's book, Pop Patraş somehow felt obliged to stand a round of drinks to everyone every time they entered Cireşica, the neighbourhood grogshop, to sip their shot glasses of Athos, a local make of brandy. Almost every evening, Pop Patraş would put the book on the grogshop table, leaving it to be browsed by curious eyes. One evening, a guy named Sile Pletosu, a homeless man who was said to have been a hardened criminal, approached the man's table. He glanced at the book and asked:

"What is this book called?"

Unaware and surprised, Pop Patraş pulled out his glasses from his pocket and read:

"Cri-me se-mi-nars…"

"Crime seminars?" Sile asked to make sure he understood correctly, his breath giving off the stench of rotten potatoes. Then, with a worried expression on his face, he went out in the street, repeating to himself: "Crime seminars."

After this seemingly unimportant event, no one in the grogshop came closer to the man's book, and Pop Patraş who was a sensitive man though, noticed this and started to wonder what might be the reason the book was called that, promising to himself to take the time to read it.

But time in the neighbourhood had little patience for people who read and especially with those who wrote. With time, the feeling of pride and joy that his son had written a book turned into a feeling of embarrassment and powerlessness, of irritation and neurosis because the student, without any explanation, filled the house with books, building towers and turrets, which were rising nastily even in the kitchen, and the books, similar to the strands of sand in a desert, brought from the student's room bits of folk songs, groans of pleasure and condoms.

At a certain moment, when a turret of books turned over the broth plates on the table, the student's mother, who was a woman of infinite gentleness, looked her husband in the eye and said:

"I think you should talk to him."

Pop Patraş entered the student's room after knocking on the door, with an office basket in one hand and a used condom in the other, and showing the condom, he told the student, in a blunt voice:

"These things should stay here," said the man, throwing the piece of rubber into the basket and leaving the basket in the student's arms.

"And from now on, I don't know how you do it, but you take all your books from this house. It's your business where you take them. We can't live like this anymore. Come and see," and the man grabbed his son by his neck and pushed him out of the room to see better a book-bound house, built in literature pages, with tunnels and corridors of book covers, and when he saw what he had done to his parents with all those books, the student had the vision of a troglodyte cave, with its wet walls of books in which the savages would cut from a shot down animal around a fire, projecting their gestures on the underground walls, stirring the restless bat colonies and the cave creatures spilling in a liquid state on the incunabula vault.

"Who gave you the money for this book?" asked the father, bringing the student with his feet to the ground, and the student, turning to his father, swallowed dryly, remembering a lady moving above him in waves of pleasure like a rider in a rodeo, with her tough breasts like two shots, jumping into a saddle in unnatural gestures as if she were going to enter the upper apartment through the ceiling.

"How many books have you sold so far?" the father asked as if in an interrogation and the student whispered, shaking his head:

"I have sold enough," and while whispering this, he could imagine all the female student and young women who had bought a book from him on the street, but he did not imagine them as a succession of faces, but instead pictured a cascade of bodies projected directly onto the bed, each woman falling, with her breasts waving like the flags of a conquered army.

"I really don't know why women buy my books," the student was saying this to a high school colleague of his who was now studying somewhere in America. "For me it is a mystery what I tell them. I don't quite remember what exactly I tell them, after I show them the book, they just suddenly come to my room and you won't believe it, they take their clothes off within seconds. It's happens unimaginably fast."

"That's fine, theoretically."

"Theoretically, it is a good thing, that's what I believe, but I am basically sad that one day I will have to marry. It would be impossible for me to marry a woman who undresses so quickly in front of a stranger who sells books. Just like the old knights, I would like my wife to wear a chastity belt and I would unlock it when I get home. But I think such a belt weighs a lot and it makes it uncomfortable to walk."

"Do you get it or not?" Pop Patraş suddenly asked, disturbing the student's memories.

"Of course, I do," the student said, starting to gather the books spread throughout his room. He gathered them all day with care, wiping off the dust, sweeping behind them, so that the house suddenly started shining like a jewel and the student's mother, Mrs Sultana Patraş, smiled at her husband who understood from her looks that he might have been too blunt with the student. The boy had already finished collecting the books within the house and quickly but carefully, he closed the door to his room because, in the slightest movement, an avalanche of books could have completely destroyed the door. In his room, all the pieces of

71

furniture, the bed, the carpet, the cabinet, the desk, the TV set, had disappeared behind a wall of books in which the student had dug kind of a niche in which he stretched as if he were in a sleeping car.

Aa, thought the student to himself, remembering the women falling in a liquid state, *I am going to sell 10 books a day, well, not really…10, let's say five, five seems to be a reasonable figure. So, the first book is supposed to be kind of a welcoming book, the second is a book of knowledge, the third one is solid, the fourth is the icing on the cake, and the fifth one is a farewell card. By selling five books a day I may get to see the sky in my room,* Andrei thought to himself, trying to walk through the books to the window. *Even today I will sell four books and the last one will be sold to Mrs Diamond*, thought the student, thinking of his female sponsor.

"Where are you going?" his worried mother asked him.

'I'm going to sell some books', the student was going to answer, but while hiding his books under his coat he corrected himself and said, "I am going for a walk."

"Okay, but take your scarf and your cap…" said the student's mother with a worried voice, watching him descend the stairs while sliding on the bumper.

When he reached the street, the student buttoned up his shirt at the neck, feeling the freezing cold.

He stopped the first woman on the street and showed her the book, trying to explain the meaning of the title to her, but this one, probably because she hadn't heard very well because of her cap, pulled her bag aside and turned a cold shoulder to the student and when she understood what he wanted she walked away in a confused state.

Towards the evening, tired and frozen, the student stopped in front of a grogshop in the neighbourhood, instinctively attracted by the heat inside. He hadn't sold a book in three hours. At some moment, he tried to sell a book to a woman with a generous breast who was driving a limousine. She thought Andrei was going to wipe her windshield at the traffic light stop and handed him some change, but he refused the money because it seemed too much. Explaining to the woman that it was about a book, the student leaned into the car too much, and when she started at the green light of the traffic light, she almost dragged the young man after her. With his feet wet, his sneakers hitting against each other, the student stopped in front of the grogshop and looked at his crimson frozen face in the window. He was maimed by the cold.

Of course, I cannot sell a book in this way, the student thought to himself, looking at his livid face and his messy hair as if it had been hidden under a sock. *I look like a bank robber*, Andrei told himself while arranging his hair, just as the door opened and his instinct pushed him inside the place.

He sat down, putting his frozen books on the table. Lifting his coat collar, he saw a beggar looking at him.

He meant to ask the beggar if he wanted a book, but he stopped when he realised it was absurd. *I would read a book*, the student thought to himself, *even if I was a beggar*.

"Why is this book called that?" the beggar who was right behind him suddenly asked. "Can you tell me?"

"Do sit down," the student invited him to the table because he had to lean back to look at the beggar. "Of course, I can tell you, I am the very author," he said, smelling rotten potatoes but suppressing his disgust very well.

"It's called *Crime Seminars* and it is based on the idea that there are two feelings that can connect two people forever in life: love and crime. Throughout their lives, two lovers are connected just like two accomplices to a crime."

"How's that?" Sile Pletosu approached the student, leaning to one side while there was absolute silence in that crowded place, because this was usually the position from which Sile was supposed to attack someone violently.

"Two accomplices to a crime remember each other throughout their lives," said the student politely. "According to the book, feelings are on the verge of extinction and with time, they disappear just like human beings disappear, meaning that they are born, grow old and die, and since love is fragile, the only genuine feeling that can bind two people forever is crime. One way or another, all the feelings left with human beings are the crime seminars."

The beggar offered the student a shot glass of Athos and the student swallowed the alcohol in one go while feeling his chest burning.

"I'll buy your book; how much is it?"

"As much as a coffee, two-point five lei."

"Then give me two," Sile said, giving the student five lei.

"Can I write an autograph for you?"

"Yes," Sile said, scrutinizing him carefully.

The student wrote an inscription on the book, but he noticed that the beggar was not too interested in it.

"Don't you want to read what I wrote on the book?"

"I am not educated, I can't read," Sile said, muttering his words.

"Then why have you just bought two of my books?"

"Let them be there. But what does your inscription say?"

Andrei explains, "I wrote, 'With goodwill and friendship!'"

Only then did the student notice that the whole room was looking to his table. He stood up, excusing himself to leave. He looked at his watch and remembered he had to meet Mrs Diamond. He had talked to her on the phone and set up a meeting at 8 pm at the company premises. He only had ten minutes left. On his way out, though, he wiped a shoulder from a nearby table and a sturdy builder as massive as a tank said, pointing to the book and handing him a five-lei note:

"Give me one too."

But since the student had no change for him, the builder bought two books, one for him and one for his friend at the table, who looked at Sile Pletosu as if he was showing a feeling of submission to him.

The student hurried out of the grog house as he wanted to make sure he kept a book for Mrs Diamond.

"I have sold four books," the student smiled to himself, running on the frozen streets and sliding on the iced patches. When he entered the company premises, he realised that it was not appropriate to ask for money for the book from the very sponsor who had financed his entire work, though. But she was in a meeting and the secretary, who knew the student, invited him in the office while the business meeting lasted unnaturally long.

Enjoying the warmth of the office, the student almost fell asleep by the time Mrs Diamond found him in the armchair. The student called this woman, who was a woman with hot breasts like two round shots ready to explode, 'Mrs Diamond' because she sold diamonds and he had forgotten her real name. The woman invited him to a couch, but it was already too late and since he had asked her for money for the book, the student did not feel much at ease and wanted to leave. Looking to the cheques on her desk, when she finally understood what the student wanted, she was going to call for her secretary, as she only had cheques and cards. When she finally found a note in her wallet, the student took it but realised he had no change, so he took the note and ran to a store, changed it and brought the change to the woman, who asked him if he didn't have time to stay longer, while meaningfully pointing to the sofa and thrusting her breasts.

Embarrassed, the student told her that he would definitely call her next week and they would meet over the weekend. He suddenly came out into the frozen street, inhaling cold air into his chest and promising to himself to never again sell a book to his sponsor. When he got home, he kissed his sleeping mother, who felt his frosty face but did not react to him being there, finally startling when she heard him crying while hitting his head on the bookshelves.

"What happened?" his mother asked him, waving aside books to reach him.

"I sold five books the whole day," the student sighed, gasping for breath while crying. "I slipped before taking the last mini-bus. I think…it was then that my banknote slipped from my pocket and I lost it."

"But I'll give you the money," his mother said, cuddling his face.

"But it's not the same thing," the student said, pulling himself out of his mother's embrace and as soon as he got out in the street, the darkness calmed him. Walking, he found himself in the centre of the town, near a theatre which an actor had just come out of and to whom two years ago he had sold a book in the street, but the actor explained to him that he was getting married and he had no money to give him for the book at that moment, but that he was going to give the money to him the following week. But every time he met the student, he noticed that the actor was avoiding him, which was why he politely and preventively asked the actor if he had read the book, indirectly reminding him of the price. The actor would tell him he had read it and he moved on. After a couple of weeks, when the student accidentally met him near the University, he ran after the actor and asked him if he liked the book, thus excluding the aesthetic pleasure.

This meant that if he liked the book, he could keep it; if he didn't like the book, he could return it. The rushed actor had answered he had liked the book, leaving the student puzzled—if he liked it and wanted to keep it, then why didn't he pay for it. Anyway, for some time, whenever he met the actor, the student didn't even get to ask him anything anymore because the actor was walked away in haste. With his soul torn out by the loss of the money on the sold books, the student watched the actor walking away as if he was aiming a gun at him and he hurried and reached him, grabbing his arm just at the moment the actor was trying to urinate.

"Hey, two years ago I gave you a book in the street. I have asked you so many times whether you liked it or not and you always delay giving me the money for it. You know something, you either give me the money for the book, or you give me the book back. It is very simple."

Surprised, the actor snatched his hand out of the student's grip, urinated, and after closing his fly, he looked at him with contempt, belching and giving off a whiff of beer. He leaned to one side and tried to hit the student, but he expected to be hit and bending his back avoided his fist, punching him back with a strong hand, so that the actor lost his balance and all the sheets of paper he had in a folder flew out and spread atop the ruins. The student helped him gather the sheets from the ground, put them in the folder and the actor, once he got on the sidewalk, took the folder and looked more carefully at the student and said:

"But you never gave me a book," said the actor, more than convinced, trying to remember, though, and the student did not get to explain to him, as he started to run, swearing as he scuttled off.

Spring had set in and the student had not sold enough books necessary to clear the way to the window of his room. He had managed to make a tunnel through which he looked at the sun just like a passenger of a plane looked through the plane window-pane. The lime trees on Domneasa Street were kissing in green songs. The swallows sprang from these branches just like tracers. In his flower-printed shirt, the student had just managed to sell a book to a beautiful girl to whom he had left her phone number as an inscription and he suddenly saw a guy who looked very much like the actor at the Dramatic Theatre and as soon as he watched him, the guy responded to his look as if he wanted to greet him. Suddenly, he said while passing.

"Hi!"

"Hi, the student replied, surprised, hurrying up to catch the guy. Excuse me, didn't I happen to give you a book I wrote, two years ago?"

"Yes, you did," said the young man.

"And have you read it," asked the student in awe.

"Yes…it was something about crime and love, right?"

"And did you like it?"

"It wasn't my type of book, but it wasn't bad either."

"But did you give me the money on it?"

"No, how much is it?"

"As much as the mini-bus fare, two-point five lei."

"Here you are, the money," said the young man, leaving the coins in the student's palm glittering just like the ships glitter in the horizon, while expected by someone castaway on a deserted island. Recalling that he was on his way to the University, the student tidied his hair and decided that he would go to classes only after admiring the Danube at least for a while that day, and so he peacefully walked down the bank of the river.